BUBBLE TROUBLE

by Nat Gabriel
illustrated by John Nez

BL 2.5 (0.5 pts)

The Kane Press
New York

Acknowledgements: Our thanks to Marc Feldman, PhD (Physics, UC Berkeley), Professor, University of Rochester and Dr. Richard Moyer, Professor of Science Education, University of Michigan—Dearborn for helping us make this book as accurate as possible.

Book Design/Art Direction: Edward Miller

Library of Congress Cataloging-in-Publication Data

Gabriel, Nat.
  Bubble trouble / by Nat Gabriel ; illustrated by John Nez.
    p. cm. — (Science solves it!)
Summary: Grace can make soap bubbles, milk bubbles, and even air bubbles (by burping) but cannot be a member of her big sister's bubble gum club until she acquires a certain skill.
  ISBN 1-57565-133-5 (pbk. : alk. paper)
  [1. Bubble gum—Fiction. 2. Bubbles—Fiction. 3. Sisters—Fiction. 4. Clubs--Fiction.] I. Nez, John A., ill. II. Title. III. Series.
  PZ7.G1156Bu 2004
  [E]—dc21

                                                      2003011697

10 9 8 7 6 5 4 3 2
First published in the United States of America in 2004 by Kane Press, Inc.
Printed in Hong Kong.

Science Solves It! is a registered trademark of Kane Press, Inc.

www.kanepress.com

"*Please*, Jane," I begged, "can I be in your club?"

"Sorry, Grace," my big sister said. "You know the rule. You have to be able to blow a bubble."

"But I can't," I said.

"Watch me," said Jane.

Jane put a piece of bubblegum in her mouth. She chewed and chewed. Then she pinched up her mouth—and blew a perfect pink bubble.

I tried. But the only thing that came out of my mouth was air and a spitty sound. "I'll never be able to do it," I said.

"Sorry," said Jane, "but that's the rule."

What's in a bubble?
If you guessed air, you are right! The air is held in by a skin. The skin of a bubble is very thin. That's one reason why bubbles pop so easily.

What's air?
Air is a gas. Gases do not have their own shapes. They spread out and fill whatever is holding them. They take its shape.

You can't see air, but you can feel it.

Keep radio on WQRS! Jane

For Jane only!

Off limits! Jane

Feed Fred fish food only. Jane

Wash hands before using! Jane

Do not read! Jane

More Science is Fun

What is a bubble?

"Bubbles. Bubbles. There must be something in this book about bubbles," I thought.

There was, but it didn't help much.

I looked at the fish bowl. Fred was blowing bubbles and that gave me an idea. All I needed was a bowl of water and a straw.

I blew some practice bubbles. Then I said, "Thanks, Fred!" and went to find Jane.

"Look, Jane!" I said. "I'm blowing bubbles! *Now* can I be in your club?"

"Our club has rules, Grace," she said.

"I thought there was only one rule—that you had to be able to blow a bubble."

"We have other rules, too," said Jane.

Jane pointed to a list. It said the bubbles had to be big and pink and last a long time.

"Your bubbles are little. You can see right through them, and they don't last," Jane said.

"Who made all these rules?" I asked.

"I did," said Jane.

BUBBLE CLUB RULES
1. Bubbles have to be big.
2. Bubbles have to last.
3. Bubbles have to be pink.

"How about a rule that says big sisters have to let little sisters in the club?" I said.

Jane put two pieces of gum in her mouth. She blew an even bigger bubble than before.

"Just keep trying, Grace," she said.

Jane and I had to go in for lunch. By now I had bubbles on the brain. So, just for fun, I tried blowing bubbles in my milk. "Look, Jane!" I said. "These bubbles last!"

"Yes, but they don't last long enough," said Jane. "Besides—"

"I know, I know. They're not pink."

Milk bubbles last longer than water bubbles because milk is stickier than water. You can try blowing bubbles in water and in milk and see the difference.

Suddenly I remembered something.
I ran upstairs to find a bag of party favors
I'd saved. I pulled out a bottle of bubble mix,
dipped the wand in, and blew. Beautiful little
bubbles floated through the air!

"*Now* can I be in your club?" I asked Jane. "Look how long my bubbles last! And the bottle is pink. Doesn't that count?"

"The bubbles are too small," Jane said. "You know the rules."

If you want bubble-mix bubbles to last longer, make them in the shade! Keeping your bubble wand really wet helps bubbles last, too.

"All you care about is rules," I told her.
"And bubbles," Jane said.

Then Jane put *three* pieces of gum in her
mouth. This time I didn't wait around to watch
her blow another perfect bubble.

I decided to take a bubble break.

"What's wrong, Grace?" asked Tom. He's my big brother.

"Jane won't let me in her club."

"So what?" he said. "All they do is blow bubbles."

"I like bubbles," I said.

"What's so great about them?" he asked.

"They're big and pink and they last," I explained.

"Not all bubbles are like that," replied Tom.

"I know," I said sadly.

"You know what's big and round and way
more fun than a bubble?" asked Tom. "A ball!"
He kicked a ball high into the air—it landed
smack on the clubhouse roof.

"Cut it out!" yelled Jane.

"Sorry, Jane!" said Tom. "Hey, how about a game of dodge ball?"

"Dodge ball is boring," said Jane. "Besides, your ball is flat." Then she put *four* pieces of gum in her mouth and blew a *huge* bubble.

"Want to help me pump?" Tom asked.

"No, thanks," I said glumly.

"Maybe lemonade will cheer you up," he said.

I was so thirsty I drank a whole cup in one gulp.

"Don't drink it too fast, Grace, or you'll—"

Tom pumps air into the ball. The air spreads out and fills the space—the same way air fills a bubble.

"*Burp!* Excuse me," I said.

We started laughing. "Burps are funny," I said.

"You know what else they are?" said Tom. "Burps are bubbles!"

"Really?"

"Yep. Air bubbles." Tom took a big gulp of lemonade—and he burped, too!

Are burps bubbles?
Yes! If you drink or eat too fast, you may swallow too much air. Pressure builds up in your stomach. When the pressure gets too great, the air either goes up through your mouth a little bit at a time, or it pops out all at once—as a burp!

I burped again. And again. And again!

Tom burped twice more. We couldn't stop laughing—or burping!

"Let's have a contest to see who can burp the loudest," Tom said.

Jane came out of her clubhouse. "What's so funny?"

"Burps!" I said. "Tom says they're bubbles."

"Grace likes my bubbles better than yours," said Tom.

"Oh, yeah?" said Jane. "Wait until she sees *this* one."

The Guinness World Record for the loudest burp is 118.1 decibels. That's about as loud as a car horn!

Jane put *five* pieces of gum in her mouth.
"Watch this," she said.
"I don't think that's a good idea," said Tom.
"It's too much gum," I told her.

But Jane didn't listen.

Her bubble got big . . . and huge . . . and humongous and . . .

The Guinness World Record for the biggest bubble-gum bubble ever blown is 23 inches across. That's almost two feet!

Pop! The bubble burst—all over Jane's face.
"Ha! Ha!" laughed Tom.
"It's not funny," Jane said. "I've got gum in
my hair! What am I going to do?"

24

"Just chop your hair off," Tom said. "I'll get the scissors."

"No!" cried Jane.

"Hold it," I said. I ran and got my book.

"It says here that peanut butter will get gum out of your hair," I said.

"Cool!" said Tom. "Can we put jelly in her hair, too?"

Jane gave him a look.

I opened the jar and got started.
"This is never going to work," said Jane.
"Sure it will," I told her. But I wasn't so sure it would, either.

But guess what? The gum came out!

"Thanks, Grace," Jane said when I was done.

"Nice work," said Tom. "But I'd still like to give her a haircut."

We ignored him.

Peanut Butter to the Rescue
So how does peanut butter get gum out of your hair? The oils in it soften the gum so that it loosens up–then you can pull it out with your fingers (or a comb). This usually works–but not always!

"Grace," Jane said, "do you still want to be in the Bubble Club?"

"Sure," I said. "But I can't because of all your rules."

"Well . . . rules can change," said Jane.

"They can?" I asked.

"Just wait and see," Jane told me.

"I like these rules much better," I said. "But don't you think we need one more?"

"You want *another* rule?" said Jane.

"Only one piece of gum at a time," I said.

"Good idea," said Jane. "I've only got one left, anyway. Want half?"

BUBBLE CLUB
RULES
1. any size
2. any kind
3. any color
4. any time

"Thanks," I said. I popped the gum in my
mouth. Then, without thinking, I stretched
it over my tongue . . . and blew a bubble!

It wasn't the biggest, or the pinkest, or
the longest lasting.

But it was mine—all mine!

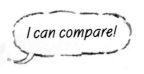

I can compare!

THINK LIKE A SCIENTIST

Grace thinks like a scientist—and so can you!

When scientists compare two objects, they try to find out how the objects are alike. They also try to find out how the objects are different.

Look Back
Look at pages 8 and 9. Describe Jane's bubble. Look at Grace's bubbles on pages 10 and 11. How do they compare to Jane's?

Try This!
You will need two kinds of bubble mix. How do they compare? Be sure to write down your findings.
• Does one wand make bigger bubbles than the other one? Why?
• Which mix feels stickier?
• Which bubbles last longer?
• Do the bubbles look alike, or different? How?

Which bubble mix do you like best? Why?

Make your own bubble mix with 1 tablespoon of glycerin, 2 tablespoons of dish soap, and 9 ounces of water!